Good Night
GIANTS

The publication has been translated and republished with permission of Verlag Jungbrunnen Wien. *Wenn ich nachts nicht schlafen kann* © 2007 by Verlag Jungbrunnen Wien.

Published by
MAGINATION PRESS
An Educational Publishing Foundation Book
American Psychological Association
750 First Street, NE
Washington, DC 20002

For more information about our books, including a complete catalog, please write to us, call 1-800-374-2721, or visit our website at www.apa.org/pubs/magination.

Printed by Worzalla, Stevens Point, Wisconsin

Library of Congress Cataloging-in-Publication Data

Janisch, Heinz.
[Wenn ich nachts nicht schlafen kann. English]
Good night giants / by Heinz Janisch ; Illustrated by Helga Bansch.
p. cm.
ISBN 978-1-4338-0950-7 (hbk.) — ISBN 978-1-4338-0951-4 (pbk.)
1. Children—Sleep—Juvenile literature. 2. Bedtime—Juvenile
literature. 3. Sleep—Juvenile literature. I. Bansch, Helga. II. Title.
BF723.S45J36 2011
613.7'94083—dc22   2010048835

Good Night GIANTS

by Heinz Janisch

Illustrated by Helga Bansch

MAGINATION PRESS • WASHINGTON, DC

American Psychological Association

When it is time to relax and get ready to sleep,
My giants and I play hide-and-go-seek.

My giants are clever and try not to be found.
Without leaving my room, I look all over town.
I look near, I look far.
I look up, I look down.
I find all my giants, those thirty-four clowns!

I find…

TWO giants
who walk on stilts

Three giants who look through scopes

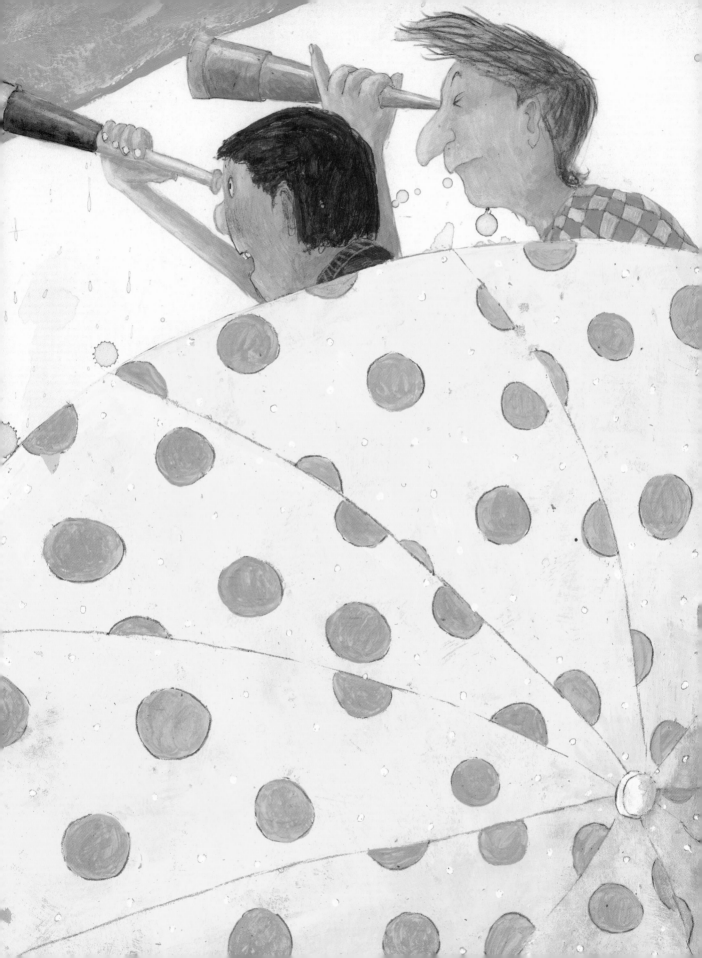

Four

giants in long-johns

Five giants with red roses

Six *giants under the piano*

Five giants traveling by ship

Four giants
in the
bathtub

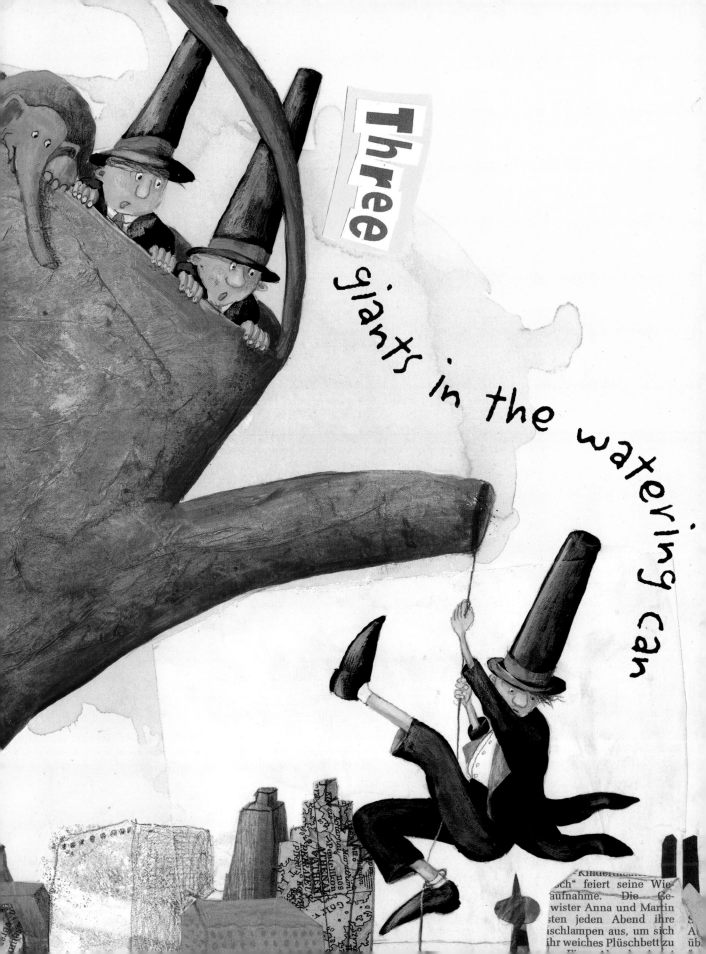

Three giants in the watering can

Two giants under a blanket

When I go off to bed,
I don't look for sheep, but instead
I look for giants all over town.

Finding the giants is a real easy task,
And once I find all my giants,
it is time to

rest and relax.

So, I call all their names, they jump to my bed.

They sing out, *Sweet dreams* and chant *good night.*

All say it together,
and that makes
things all right.

THE GIANTS' SONG

Wiggle out your energy
to get ready to sleep.

Put happy thoughts in your head
and peace in your feet,

Now, take a deep breath
and blow out the air.

Float with its sound,
but wait,
you're not there.

Do that again.

And again and again, a couple more times,

Keep breathing and relaxing
for each thought in your mind.

NOTE TO PARENTS

by Michael A. Tompkins, PhD

Parents tend to sleep well when their children sleep well. Fortunately, for most kids and parents, things work out just fine. In large part, this is because sleep is hardwired. That is, your child's brain will get the sleep necessary to help him or her develop into a vital and healthy human being. However, that is not to say that your child's environment—particularly parents—doesn't play an important role in sleep, too. Here are a few suggestions for parents who want to help their child develop and master the skills necessary to maintain an adequate amount of sleep throughout his or her life.

WHAT YOU CAN DO

Build a bedtime routine.

A bedtime routine signals your child's brain that sleep time is coming. In addition, children, particularly young children, are comforted by a predictable bedtime routine, which lowers a child's anxiety at night. However, families don't all operate on the same timetable. Some parents have long commutes home and dinner may not get on the table until 7 p.m. or later, which means that in spite of their best efforts, their children don't get to bed until 9 p.m. or so. Take heart. It is less important what time your child's bedtime routine begins, so long as it begins about the same time every night. If more often than not, you get your children in bed by 9 p.m., set that as the beginning of your child's bedtime routine. Similarly, strive for a regular awakening time, particularly if your child has trouble settling down at night. A regular awakening time, even when your child was awake later than usual, ensures that sleep will come on time and perhaps a bit earlier the next night.

Build in transition time.

Children benefit from a transition period before bed. Sing to your child her favorite songs and then read to her for 15 minutes. This book, and the Giants Song at the end of the story, are meant to be part of a normal bedtime routine, and fit well in this transition period. Give your child a 5-minute back massage or play a quick eyes-closed game, like tracing letters or words on each other's backs and guessing what was written. Savoring is a wonderful eyes-closed transition exercise too: Lie in bed with your child and review your day with her, highlighting the positive and wonderful—savoring each—then ask your child to do the same. Savor the flutter of leaves as they fell to the sidewalk during the walk to school. Savor the crispness of the green apples she had for a snack or the fun game she played with her best friend. Any soothing or calming activity is great. Sing to your child the song at the end of this book and make it part of your child's transition time. In addition, insist that your child stop any activity that involves a screen (television, computers, and video games) for at least 30 minutes before bedtime.

Don't tell your child to "go to sleep."

We all do it, but we cannot control sleep. In

other words, we don't "go" to sleep. Sleep comes to us. If your child is anxious or eager to please you, commanding your child to do something she cannot control may make her anxious and it may be more difficult for sleep to come. Instead, encourage your child to do what she can control—to lay quietly in her bed and wait. If your child is tossing and turning, encourage her to cope quietly using a soothing strategy, such as singing to herself or savoring, and reassure her that sleep will come.

Don't talk about your sleep or ask about your child's sleep.

Children are listening and learning from parents all the time. Parents who don't sleep well can teach their child to become anxious about sleep or unknowingly set unrealistic and unhelpful expectations about sleep. Children may learn to believe that every night's sleep should be sound and deep or that terrible things might happen if they don't sleep well. Don't ask your child, "How did you sleep last night?" or talk much about your own restless night. If you want to talk about your sleep with your partner, do so when your children are not around. Instead, de-focus on sleep within your home. If your child complains that he didn't sleep well, remind him that sleep has a mind of its own and that tonight sleep likely will come a bit easier because it took a bit longer to come last night.

You can de-focus on sleep at nights, too. A well-rested and calm parent is the best parent to help a child who awakens at night. A sleep-deprived parent may be frustrated that the child has awakened him again or too anxious to get back to sleep to give the child sufficient care and attention. Your child may notice this and become over

anxious and clingy. When possible, share the duty of attending to a restless kid.

Go to your child's bed— don't bring her to yours.

If your child awakens at night and comes to your room for comfort, take her back to her own bed and lay down with her there. Try not to bring a restless child into your bed. You are less likely to awaken your child when you ease out of her bed than when you carry her from your bed to hers and then tuck her in. Even if your child is not feeling well, it is better to lay with your child in her bed. You always want to associate your child's bed, not your own, with soothing and sleep. If you love snuggle time with your child, welcome your child into your bed in the morning where you can snuggle, read the comics, or just hang out for some one-on-one time.

With a parent's help, most children develop sleep habits that contribute to happy and healthy kids. However, some children may have persistent problems with sleep because they are anxious or depressed; they have a sleep disorder, such as sleep apnea; or they have some other physical or psychological condition. If your child continues to have significant difficulties falling asleep and staying asleep through the night, speak first with your child's pediatrician and then consult with a mental health professional with expertise in treating sleep problems.

Michael A. Tompkins, PhD, is a licensed psychologist and specializes in cognitive–behavior therapy for anxiety and mood disorders in adults, adolescents, and children. Dr. Tompkins is the author of several books, including My Anxious Mind: A Teen's Guide to Managing Anxiety and Panic, *co-authored with Katherine Martinez, PsyD.*

ABOUT THE AUTHOR

Heinz Janisch writes children's books and books for adults.
Janisch has received several literary awards, including
the 1998 Austrian prize for promoting children's literature.

ABOUT THE ILLUSTRATOR

Helga Bansch attended the Pedagogical Academy in Graz,
where she trained as a primary school teacher. She worked with
children with behavioral issues and discovered painting as a
means of expression. Since then, Bansch has focused on painting
pictures with acrylic on paper or canvas; illustrating children's
books; and making dolls, puppets, and objects of sandstone,
clay, and papier-mâché.